W9-BKM-893

My "t" Sound Box®

(Blends are included in this book.)

Library of Congress Cataloging-in-Publication Data
Moncure, Jane Belk.
My "t" sound box / by Jane Belk Moncure; illustrated by Colin King.
p. cm.
Summary: A little boy fills his sound box with many words beginning with the letter "t."
ISBN 1-56766-786-4 (lib. reinforced : alk. paper)
[1. Alphabet.] I. King, Colin, ill. II. Title.
PZ7.M739 Myt   2000
[E]—dc21   99-056567

My "t"
Sound Box®

Jane Belk Moncure

illustrated by Colin King

The Child's World®

Little  had a box.

"I will find things that begin
with my 't' sound," he said.

"I will put them into
my sound 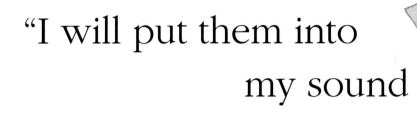 box."

"I like toys.
I will look for toys."

Little  t found a toy train

on a train track.

Did he put the toy train and
the track into his box? He did.

Little  found a toy tractor.

Did he put the tractor into the box with the toy train and the track?

 He did.

Then Little  t found a truck.

He drove that truck up, up, up

a tall mountain.

He drove to the top,
the very tip-top!

At the top of the tall mountain,
he found two turtles.

Did he put the two
turtles into his box?
He did.

Then he found

a toad.

Did he put the toad
into the box? He did.

Now the box was so full that he could not see over the top.

He tripped.

He tumbled down,

down,

down the mountain.

He tumbled into a turkey.

Turkey feathers flew!

So Little t made a
turkey-feather hat.

He and the turkey danced together.

Little  found a tambourine.

He tapped the tambourine,

"Tap, tap, tap.
Tap, tap, tap."

Little  t, the turkey,

and the toad
danced some more.

Then he put all of
his things into the box.

Suddenly, Little  heard a terrific noise!

He ran . . .

into a tent.

When he looked out, he saw a

tiger.

The tiger opened its mouth.
There were many

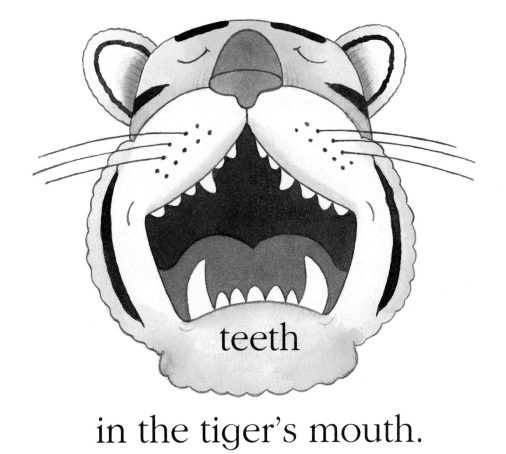

teeth

in the tiger's mouth.

"I have a loose tooth," said the tiger.
"Please pull out my tooth."

So Little  pulled out the tooth.

"Thank you," said the tiger.

Then Little  t and the tiger went inside the tent.

They played with all the toys in the box.

toad

tambourine

truck

tractor

two turtles

turkey

tent

tiger

train

train track

They had a terrific time!

Can you read these words with Little  ?

telephone

tulip

tray

tricycle

toe

tree

tomato

toothbrush

television

tie

table

top

taco

tire

teapot

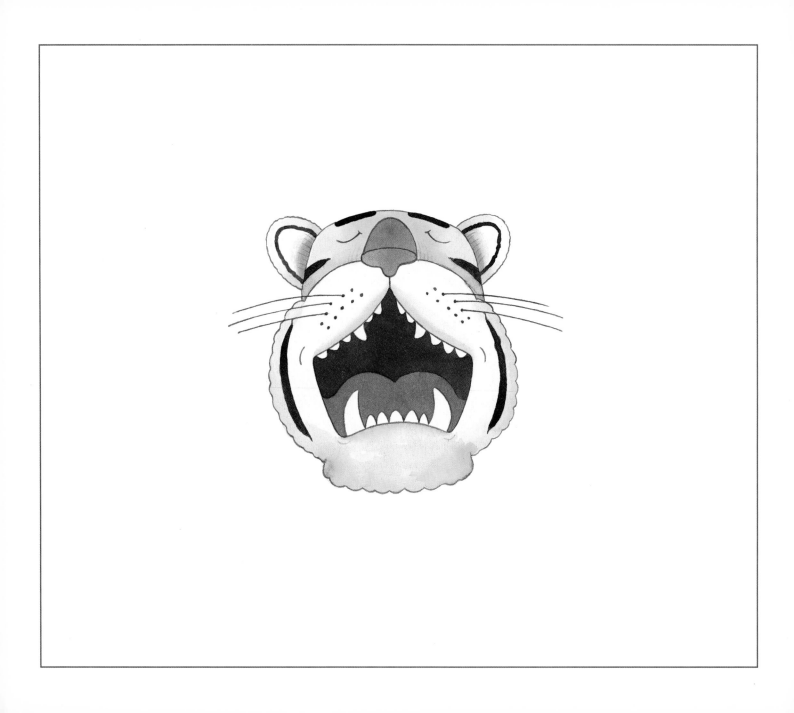

ABOUT THE AUTHOR AND ILLUSTRATOR

Jane Belk Moncure began her writing career when she was in kindergarten. She has never stopped writing. Many of her children's stories and poems have been published, to the delight of young readers, including her son Jim, whose childhood experiences found their way into many of her books.

Mrs. Moncure's writing is based upon an active career in early childhood education. A recipient of an M.A. degree from Columbia University, Mrs. Moncure has taught and directed nursery, kindergarten, and primary grade programs in California, New York, Virginia, and North Carolina. As a former member of the faculties of Virginia Commonwealth University and the University of Richmond, she taught prospective teachers in early childhood education.

Mrs. Moncure has travelled extensively abroad, studying early childhood programs in the United Kingdom, The Netherlands, and Switzerland. She was the first president of the Virginia Association for Early Childhood Education and received its award for outstanding service to young children.

A resident of North Carolina, Mrs. Moncure is currently a full-time writer and educational consultant. She is married to Dr. James A. Moncure, former vice president of Elon College.

Colin King studied at the Royal College of Art, London. He started his freelance career as an illustrator, working for magazines and advertising agencies.

He began drawing pictures for children's books in 1976 and has illustrated over sixty titles to date.

Included in a wide variety of subjects are a best-selling children's encyclopedia and books about spies and detectives.

His books have been translated into several languages, including Japanese and Hebrew. He has four grown-up children and lives in Suffolk, England, with his wife, three dogs, and a cat.